Cool pants to the Rescue

by Charlie Nunn and Karen London

A Series of Adventures from Sweetville
Book One

More adventures from Sweetville:

Book 2: Where are you Mr Sticky?

Coming Soon!

Cool pants to the Rescue

by Charlie Nunn and Karen London

Published by
Sweetville Press

Copyright: Sweetville Press
email: sweetvillepress@live.co.uk

First Published in 2010 by Sweetville Press
Cool Pants to the Rescue by Charlie Nunn & Karen London
Edited & Illustrated by Janet Nunn

ISBN: 978-0-9565281-0-0

Designed and typeset by Sweetville Press
Printed by CPI Antony Rowe, Chippenham, Wiltshire.

Cool Pants to the Rescue

by Charlie Nunn and Karen London

Published by Sweetville Press

Contents

Chapter 1: The cleverest sweet 9

Chapter 2: Into the Wild Wurly Woods 19

Chapter 3: Ghosts aren't real . . are they? 35

Chapter 4: Visiting Professor Ice 'n' Stein 45

Chapter 5: The Old Sweets Home 59

Chapter 6: Sounds like a plan to me 71

Chapter 7: Cool Pants to the Rescue 91

Chapter 1:

The cleverest sweet

At number 13 Sweetwrapper Lane, Toppety and Treaclepops were busy watching television. It was their favourite programme, 'Who wants to win a lot of money?'. They never missed it. Treaclepops was doing a handstand up against the wall and Toppety was on the edge of the sofa thinking . . thinking . . thinking.

"Mint Allstrong!" he shouted at the TV.

"No, you're wrong, Toppety, Mint Allstrong was the first sweet on the moon. The question is: Who was the first sweet in space?"

Treaclepops concentrated more intently on her handstand. "Look at me Toppety, what do you think of my handstand?"

Toppety didn't hear her, he was too busy thinking . . thinking . . thinking, trying to think of the answer .... "Chewy Wivnutzin!" he shouted.

"Yes, that's right Toppety! If you'd actually been on the show you'd have won big time. Perhaps one day you'll get on the show and win a lot of money."

"Where's my drink Treaclepops? I need some refreshment before I answer the next question."

Just then the doorbell rang.

"You get it Toppety, I'm doing the longest handstand I've ever done, and I don't even feel woozy yet!"

"Oh, all right, do I have to do everything around

here ...."

Toppety jumped from the sofa, ran to the door, opened it and couldn't see anyone.

"I'm down here ...!"

It was Toppety's friend, Licky Lolly. To Toppety's amazement, Licky seemed to be kneeling in a puddle of pink water. Then Toppety realised that Licky wasn't kneeling at all - Licky *was* the pink puddle.

"I'm melting Toppety! Help me!"

"My word Licky you are in trouble, of course I can help!" And with that, Toppety ran to the kitchen and looked for the big spoon and the bucket.

Hearing all the frantic running about, Treaclepops flipped back on to her feet, and was now at the front door trying to keep Licky calm.

"I'm disappearing Treaclepops! Where's Toppety? He'd better hurry ... I'm melting fast!"

Toppety reappeared, the big spoon and bucket in his hands. "Here Treaclepops, you hold the bucket and I'll scoop up Licky with the big spoon."

They carefully scooped and scooped until all of Licky was in the bucket.

"Now let's get her to the freezer fast," said Toppety. "You'll be all right Licky, I promise."

Licky was melting fast, but just before she oozed into liquid form, she managed to tell Toppety and Treaclepops what was happening in Lolly Town, and why she'd risked everything to get to them.

"We're all melting!" she cried. "It started about

a week ago, when we began noticing little puddles of coloured water all over town. Then, Professor Ice'n'Stein Lolly, our scientist, discovered that it was us, *we* were making the puddles, *we* were melting. Everyone is staying in, we daren't go out, we're all very frightened. Professor Ice'n'Stein sent me to you to see if you can come and help us. He asked me, because he knew I was the fastest best runner, as last week I won the Lolly Running Fast Heats for Lolly Town. We are asking for your help because we know you are very clever Toppety, and you are the best at handstands Treaclepops. We know you won't let us down."

Licky was barely recognizable now, just a pink puddle in a bucket! Treaclepops quickly opened the freezer door and slid Licky into an ice cube tray.

"Sorry Licky, this is all I've got to put you in at the moment. You'll be safe now, till we find out what's going on in Lolly Town. Don't worry, everything'll be okay, I know it will."

"Let's go!" cried Toppety enthusiastically. "We've got a whole town of lollies to save!"

"We'd best wrap up well Toppety, it's chilly in Lolly Town, and we don't want to catch a cold."

"And you had better put some shoes on Treaclepops, it might get sticky on our trip!"

Treaclepops ran up the stairs, rushed into the bedroom and opened her shoe cupboard. Pink, yellow, red, green, mauve, blue, turquoise, aqua-marine, soft scarlet, light scarlet and deep scarlet and many, many more colours, high-heels, flat shoes, wedges, flip-flops, high-back sandals, sling-back sandals, ankle boots, knee boots and thigh-length boots! It was as if they were all shouting "Wear me!" Of course, some shoes were more polite than others, the high-heels were awfully well spoken in contrast to the sling-back sandals who were as common as muck, you wouldn't believe the bad language, and the thigh-length boots ...?! Well, we won't go into that, but they were very rude!

"What are you doing Treaclepops?"

"I won't be a moment," she shouted back from inside the cupboard, still trying to decide which shoes to wear. Then Treaclepops remembered that the pink ankle boots were 'non-stick' boots, and didn't Toppety say it might get sticky? She hastily put them on and ran back down the stairs to meet Toppety, who was already waiting at the front door in his jacket and hat.

And so they set off, wondering what they would find and what adventures were in store.

At the edge of Sweetville was the sign post to Lolly Town.

There was an arrow pointing to 'The Long, Safe Way', and another pointing to 'The Short, But Dangerous Way'.

"Toppety, we always go the long, safe way."

"Yes I know, Treaclepops, but this time lollies lives are at stake. I think we had better take the short, but dangerous way, because there is no time to lose!"

"But that means going through the Wild Wurly Woods. Everyone says that it's dark and scary in there, and that's where Chocco Rocko and his gang The Wild Wurlies hang out."

Treaclepops looked a bit scared, and immediately did a handstand against a nearby tree. She had a habit of doing handstands when she was feeling anxious and afraid.

"It's going to be alright Treaclepops, but we can't hang about, the lollies need our help."

Hearing Toppety's comforting words, Treaclepops returned to her feet.

"Ah, I see you've got your non-sticky boots on Treaclepops," he said as they flashed past his nose. "You'll probably need those. Dipsy Sherbert told me that it's sticky in the Wurly Woods, and the last thing we want to do is get stuck in any sticky situations."

"Come on then, let's go!" said Treaclepops. She closed her eyes and took a deep breath. "I'm scared Toppety, hold my hand."

Toppety walked over and gave her a big, big, hug. This always helped. "We'll be okay Treaclepops, don't be frightened, I'm here with you."

Toppety took her hand and they walked together towards the Wild Wurly Woods.

Chapter 2:

Into the Wild Wurly Woods

As the two friends stepped into the Wild Wurly Woods, they glanced at each other and hesitated. Ahead looked very dark, gloomy and dank. There was a sweet, sickly, stench in the air. It seemed to hang over them.

Treaclepops pinched her nose tightly.

"Phewy!" she exclaimed. "What is that horrid, horrid smell?"

"I've no idea, Treaclepops," replied Toppety.

Treaclepops gripped his hand tightly, very tightly indeed.

"Ouch!" he yelped, rubbing his hands against

his jacket to ease the pain. "That hurt!"

"I'm sorry, I'm sorry!" Treaclepops looked startled. "I didn't mean to hurt you." Treaclepops leaned her head on Toppety's shoulder. "I don't like this one bit. Can we turn back and take the long, safe way?"

"No, Treaclepops, we're here now, and we have to carry on. We don't have much time."

Treaclepops peered down at her pink non-sticky ankle boots. She wondered why she couldn't see them any more. Her boots had disappeared!

"Oh Toppety! I seem to be sinking into some gooey toffee sticky stuff!"

"You won't get stuck. The advert said these boots are 'absolutely non-stickable'. Hold on Treaclepops, I'll lift you up out of the gooey toffee sticky stuff ..."

But, before he could get a grip on her, Treaclepops panicked. Thinking that she was going to sink out of sight, she flipped herself over and did a handstand.

"Oh Treaclepops! Now you are well and truly stuck. Your *boots* are non-stick but your *hands* aren't!"

Now, instead of sinking, Treaclepops was stuck fast. No matter how hard she tried, she couldn't lift her hands out of the gooey toffee sticky stuff. Toppety managed to reach over and grab her legs, but even he could not pull her free. Her hands were stuck firm.

"Try again Toppety! Please! I'm frightened." Toppety leaned over once more, and held on to Treaclepops' legs tightly.

"Now, get ready - I'm going to give one almighty

pull. Ready ... one ...two ..three .. PULL!"

Toppety's hands slipped, and he was catapulted back, falling in a heap against a tree. "Well, that didn't work did it! I'll have to think of some other way to get you out."

Toppety thought for a minute or two. He was sitting up against the tree and had taken off his shoes. He always had good ideas when he took off his shoes. He didn't know why, but it always seemed to be the case. He'd often thought this was odd, but had grown to accept it. Toppety remembered how he had been sitting in his workshop one day with just his socks on, when he invented the idea that having your pudding before your dinner was preferable, and, that if you had two puddings, you wouldn't need your dinner at all.

"I've got it!" he cried. "I'll go home and make a small, portable crane out of those old egg boxes, soap powder packets and those very handy, all-purpose empty washing-up liquid bottles. Oh, and that long piece of string that Dipsy Sherbert gave me will come in handy as well ...."

"No Toppety! You can't leave me here on my own! I'm scared. What if Chocco Rocko and his Wild Wurlies should come along?"

"Yeah, I never thought of that, of course I can't leave you here alone. I haven't got time to go home and build a crane. That was a stupid idea." And with that, Toppety put his shoes back on.

Toppety walked around Treaclepops, eyeing up the sticky situation. "This is just the kind of sticky situation I was hoping to avoid," he muttered. "You know you've only got yourself to blame Treaclepops, but I would never leave you in a pickle like this one, I would never do that."

"What's that noise Toppety?"

"What noise? I can't hear anything."

"Listen .. it sounds like ..."

"What? Cats having a loud argument about dogs?"

"No. Not exactly .."

"Dogs having a loud argument about cats?"

"No, not cats or dogs! It's more of a ....."

"Squirrels having a loud argument about whose nuts belong to whom ...."

"blah blah blah nuts..."

"Shut up Toppety! Now you're just being stupid! I think we are in trouble, if that is Chocco Rocko coming ...."

A loud whirring, clattering, whirling noise began to get louder and louder and closer and closer, until, Toppety and Treaclepops could hardly hear themselves think.

"Toppety, I can hardly hear myself think!" cried Treaclepops at the top of her voice!

But Toppety couldn't hear her. He was busy staring at the two bikes that were whirling and hurtling towards them! "Oh fudge! It is Chocco Rocko and that's Caramella on the other bike. What are we going to do now?"

Chocco Rocko and his girlfriend Caramella soon arrived. Chocco did a whirl and a wheelie. Caramella stopped near Toppety and slowly swept her hair back into position, checking herself in the handlebar mirror.

"He's such a big show-off!" Toppety whispered under his breath thinking Caramella couldn't hear him.

He was startled when she replied. "Yes he is a big show-off, that's why I like him, but you know I've got a soft centre for you, don't you Toppety?"

Toppety's cheeks blushed bright red!

"Well, that's all well and nice Caramella, but Treaclepops is in trouble, and I've got to get her out of that gooey toffee sticky stuff."

Treaclepops was beginning to feel a little light headed, all the sugar had rushed to her head. Caramella looked disinterested, pulled a yoyo from her pocket and began to play with it. Chocco Rocko was still whirling around on his bicycle.

"Well hello sweet Treaclepops .. and .. Thing-eme-pop? Moppety ain't it?" Chocco came to a skid stop very near to where Treaclepops was stuck.

"It's Toppety! My name's Toppety!"

"Of course it is . . . Floppety . . . my mistake!" Chocco laughed.

Caramella giggled. Even Treaclepops let out a tiny "Tee hee!"

Toppety tried to ignore Chocco, he had more important things to think about.

"Don't worry Treaclepops, I'm thinking." He glanced over at Caramella who was doing a 'walk the dog' with her yoyo. It was a very difficult trick, but Caramella seemed to have mastered it quite well, he thought. Just then a brilliant idea popped into his head.

"I've got a brilliant idea!" cried Toppety. "We could use the string from the yoyo to lasso your legs Treaclepops, and pull you out of the gooey toffee sticky stuff with pedal power."

"I don't care how you do it Toppety! Just get me out of here. This has been one of my worst hand-stands *ever!*"

Caramella looked huffy. "You're not using my yoyo!" she said with a huff. "The string might break."

Chocco Rocko quickly pointed to Toppety's hat. "I want that!" he exclaimed, "or we won't help you!"

Toppety loved his hat. It had chrome and glass goggles attached. He always wore it when he was riding around on his bicycle. It stopped the wind from blowing in his eyes so they wouldn't water, and that was very important, because you need to see where you're going when you're riding a bicycle. The goggles had little wipers for when it was raining! But if it was the only way of getting Treaclepops free, then he was willing to sacrifice his hat. Toppety took it off, and with great ceremony handed it over to Chocco Rocko.

"Thanks Ploppety!" Chocco smirked, and put on his new hat.

Caramella looked cross. "It's *my* yoyo," she blurted out crossly. "I want those pink boots!"

"She can't have my pretty pink boots!" cried Treaclepops wiggling her feet.

"But Treaclepops .." pleaded Toppety, "it's the only way you're going to get out. I've already given up my hat for you."

"Oh alright! I suppose I'll have to," whimpered Treaclepops.

Caramella quickly whipped the pink boots from Treaclepops' feet. She did one last trick on her yoyo, then handed it to Toppety. He couldn't resist showing off his own yoyo skills and did a quick 'loop the loop'.

"TOPPETY!" yelled Treaclepops. "My head's dizzy, stop showing off, nobody's impressed!" Treaclepops looked annoyed.

Caramella looked impressed. "Toppety, you should join me for The Sweet Allcomers Yoyo Championship Competition, you are really good."

"I might, if there's a prize!"

Toppety loved competitions,
and he knew he was a whizz with a yoyo.

"I'm pretty good too you know ..." said the upside down Treaclepops. "I could whip both of you with one hand tied behind my back."

"Now who's showing off, and I'd like to see you try it, perhaps a blindfold too eh?" Toppety grinned, as he unravelled the string, tied one end to the back of Caramella's bicycle, and the other end to Treaclepops' feet.

"This is never going to work," mocked Chocco, doing another wheelie and a skidded stop, causing a bit of mud from his wheel to skip up and hit Toppety square on his bottom.

Toppety bent down and dipped his hand into the very edge of the gooey toffee sticky stuff. He pulled out a lovely gooey mess, rolled it into a ball, and threw it powerfully at Chocco who was still laughing. His mouth was wide open when it took the full force of the gooey ball! The toffee rocket knocked Chocco off his bike and on to the ground.

"Yes!" cried Toppety! "It was a big target though, couldn't really miss could I?"

"Oh my poor Choccy Woccy!" cried Caramella, "let me kiss it better!" Caramella ran over to where her 'Choccy Woccy' lay, and tended to her fallen sweetie. Toppety climbed on to Caramella's bicycle. "Hold tight Treaclepops .. get ready .. one, two, three . . . Let's Go!"

Toppety pedalled and pedalled. He could hear the whirring of the wheels as he fought to free Treaclepops. Then suddenly with an almighty Sch-clop! Treaclepops was sucked out of the gooey toffee sticky stuff, flew over Toppety's head, and landed comfortably on her bottom on a very convenient mound of soft long grass.

"Ahh . . . that's better . . . I thought I was going

to be stuck in there till the cows came home . . . what a relief!" sighed Treaclepops, as she watched Toppety fly past her at what seemed like 200 miles an hour!

Toppety put on the brakes, but this only aided in the bicycle's flipperty-flip, and Toppety was flying through the air head over heels, spinning and twirling. He came down with a heavy thud on his bottom on a hard dirt mound!

"Ouch! Just my luck!" he cried, brushing the dirt from his backside. "Let's go Treaclepops! We'd better make a move while 'Choccy Woccy' over there is still a bit woozy!"

Toppety and Treaclepops ran past Chocco and Caramella . . . and went deeper into the woods.

Chapter 3:

Ghosts aren't real . . are they?

"Well, we sorted out big, bad 'Choccy Woccy' didn't we Treaclepops? He's not all that is he! We'll have to get a move on, that sticky situation you got us into has set us back a bit."

"Well, I didn't mean to get stuck did I?" said Treaclepops defiantly. "How was I to know the gooey toffee sticky stuff was *that* sticky!"

"Well, it is called gooey toffee sticky stuff for a reason, Treaclepops!"

"They should put up a warning sign," complained Treaclepops.

"Come on," said Toppety, "we'd better hurry."

The more they ran the darker the wood became. Each step and skip took them further into the darkness. Then they saw a sign post up ahead, it simply read 'Dead Centre Wurly Woods'.

"Well at least we know we are half way to Lolly Town. What an adventure we are having Treaclepops."

"Yes, but I'm scared Toppety, look my hands are shaking, my teeth are chattering and my knees are a-knocking."

Toppety looked at Treaclepops, and sure enough her hands were shaking, her teeth were chattering and her knees were a-knocking. Toppety could see she needed a big cuddle, so he wrapped his arms around her and squeezed her tight.

"Is that better Treaclepops?" he asked, rubbing his hands up and down her back to try and warm her up.

"Yes that's lovely, thanks. I feel a lot better now. Shall we keep going?"

Toppety kept hold of her hand as they carried on. They could see a small clearing just beyond the trees. There was a murky mist hovering above the ground.

"Oh, I hope that's not what it looks like Toppety. Tell me it isn't!"

"I can't really make it out," he replied, hoping upon hope that it wasn't what he thought it was.

But as they got closer, white headstones started appearing through the murk . . . it was a graveyard!

"Oh Toppety! Now I'm *really* frightened! I hate spooky places, and there might be lots of ghostly goin's on!"

"Don't be silly Treaclepops, ghosts aren't real, they're a figment of our imagination. When we die we go to heaven and that's where we live. We don't die and decide to hang around graveyards, that's silly talk! Now let's be brave!"

"Does everybody go to heaven Toppety?"

"Yes, Treaclepops, everyone goes to heaven. It doesn't matter if you're a sweet, a lolly or a cake, everybody goes to heaven."

"Even if you've been bad?"

"Oh yes! even if you've been bad, heaven is very forgiving!"

Treaclepops felt reassured by that comforting thought. "C'mon then Toppety, let's go!" she said bravely.

They put their best feet forward and off they marched towards the mist and into the murk. They reached the first headstone, it read, 'Gone, but not forgotten.' They passed the next, it read, 'Gone, but still 'ere!' The third read, 'Gone with the wind! but forever up our noses'.

"Touching eh?" said Toppety, wiping a tear from his eye.

There were many headstones of all shapes and sizes. Some were old, they were crumbling away at the edges and draped in a sort of green slimy stuff. Others had inscriptions that were barely visible.

Toppety nudged Treaclepops, and tugged at her sleeve to slow her down.

"Look at this one Treaclepops ...."

Treaclepops didn't want to stop, never mind stop and read too!

"What is it, what is it?" she said, anxiously looking about her, just in case some THING jumped out at her. "I can't stop Toppety, I'm too scared to stop Toppety, we've got to get out of here."

They kept on going. Headstones were popping up everywhere, to the left and to the right. 'My friend Chewy, he came to a sticky end' . . 'Cola Bottle, his fizz went flat too soon' . .

Then they stopped dead in their tracks.

GONE with THE WIND! but FOREVER UP OUR NOSES

Treaclepops couldn't have been any closer to Toppety if she tried, she was almost in his jacket with him.

"Did you hear that, Toppety?" she whispered, leaning her head on his shoulder.

"Hear what?" he asked.

"I heard a low groaning noise, like someone was in pain . . ."

"That was me Treaclepops, you're standing on

my foot!"

They carried on walking. The mist and murk was turning into fog, it was murkier than ever.

Toppety suddenly stopped once again. "Can you hear that knocking? Sounds like someone's knocking, trying to get out of their coffin . . ."

"That's my knees a-knocking!" Treaclepops whispered, quietly pointing at her knees.

"Oh yes so it is!" Toppety laughed with relief as he surveyed her knocking knees.

They walked on into the fog. Every little sound, every twig that snapped under their feet made them jump, even the rustle of their own clothes made them feel uneasy.

Toppety picked up some pace, he thought he heard noises, and could see shadows in the fog creeping from every direction.

"Hey Toppety wait for me!" cried Treaclepops, as she started to run too, her socks splashing in the puddles as she hopped, skipped and jumped. They were side by side running scared. "I can see a gate Toppety, there, just past that big statue."

They ran beyond the statue and through the big heavy iron gates. They stopped and looked back. The fog had lifted and disappeared. They both gazed at the elegant statue. A beautiful white angel, who looked down at them, with what seemed to be a reassuring smile.

"She's making sure all the ghosts stay in the graveyard and don't come out and scare people," said Toppety, tying up his shoe lace.

"But I thought you said there were no such things

as ghosts Toppety?"

"I think there might be *now* Treaclepops, after all that!"

They turned around and they could see a sign just a few yards away. It read: 'Welcome to Lolly Town'.

"Let's go Toppety, we've made it!"

They walked into Lolly Town, hand in hand, feeling very triumphant and pleased with themselves.

Chapter 4:

Visiting Professor Ice 'n' Stein

Treaclepops and Toppety stood nervously on the doorstep of Professor Ice 'n' Stein's house. This is where Licky Lolly had told them they must come. They had never met the Professor, but they knew he had the reputation of being an eccentric. The house was rather grand, and there was a large shiny plaque on the huge front door, with the words: 'Professor Ice 'n' Stein ICEWIZ' emblazoned upon it in big gold letters.

Treaclepops was pooped. She looked as though she had run the Sweetville Choclathon twice. Her pretty golden hair now hung like limp spaghetti strands, and she was covered down to her feet in caked-on gooey toffee sticky stuff. Treaclepops was still upset about Caramella having her pink non-sticky boots. She stared dizzily down at her once immaculate, but now soggy, strawberry pink socks. They were barely visible underneath all the gunge.

Toppety looked up, and found what he thought must be the doorbell. He reached forward and tugged on the enormous pulley. Just as he did, some jolly music filled the air. A slight smile crept across Treaclepops' face, and she started tapping her feet and swinging her hips from side to side.

"He's got good taste in music hasn't he?" she said, as Toppety grabbed her by the hand and started whirling her around.

"Groovy ain't it!" said Toppety, humming along.

Treaclepops began to sing. "It makes my heart go flippety-flop .... de, do, do, dooo ..."

Just at that instant, the door burst open wide, and a very flustered looking lolly came rushing out waving his arms around. He was wearing the most blindingly multi-coloured over-sized overalls that Treaclepops had ever seen.

"Take cover .. it's going to BLOW!" he yelled, as he flew past them and dived into the nearest bush.

Toppety and Treaclepops looked at each other in horror and promptly followed him head first into the foliage.

"It's a catastrophe!" Professor Ice 'n' Stein spluttered, his hair springing about and coiled like springs. "I knew I shouldn't have put the wotsit in with the oojamaflip ... and now it's too late!" From waving his arms in the air in dismay, he clasped his hands tightly over his ears. Toppety and Treaclepops did the same, and they all waited for the inevitable big bang.

They waited and waited. Nothing happened.

"Did you hear it?" the Professor asked removing one hand from his ear.

"Not yet," replied Toppety. "I didn't hear anything except my head pounding."

Treaclepops looked puzzled. "I haven't heard anything either," she said, "but my ears are stuffed full of gooey toffee sticky stuff." She tilted her head, stuck her finger in her ear, and waggled it about.

The Professor looked bewildered. "That's a relief then," he said, as he scrambled on all fours out of the greenery. He stood up and brushed the leaves and twigs from his clothes.

"That was a lucky escape. If you don't put the wotsit in the right place, you usually end up with a big explosion. We could have been blown to smitheroons."

"And smithereens," giggled Treaclepops.

The Professor removed his eyeball, held it up, polished it on his sleeve until it was gleaming and popped it back into his eye socket. Toppety and Treaclepops looked at each other in surprise. They'd never seen a lolly do that before, or even a sweet for that matter!

"Don't worry about me eye-ee, me heartees," the Professor said, imitating a pirate for a second. "There's more strange things going on around here than that!"

Toppety and Treaclepops followed the Professor into his house.

"Come in, come in!" he said. "You caught me at a bad moment, the wotsit I was experimenting with wasn't up to scratch. It was second rate. I should never have trusted Luvly Jubbly to get me my wotsits. He's dodgy at the best of times. And now I've got to start all over again with a new wotsit ... you don't know where I can get a decent wotsit from I suppose?"

Treaclepops and Toppety looked at each other, and then at the Professor.

"No, I've never seen a wotsit in Sweetville," said Toppety.

The Professor turned away and rustled through

some papers on his desk.

Treaclepops looked at Toppety strangely. "What's a wotsit Toppety?" she whispered.

"I don't know," Toppety whispered back. "I'm trying to pretend that I know what a wotsit is so the Professor doesn't think I'm stupid."

"I thought you two would never get here," the Professor said, still looking through his papers. He glanced at Treaclepops. "And you look like you could do with a wash young lady. How did you get covered in all that gooey toffee sticky stuff?"

"It's a long story," said Treaclepops. "And it's why it has taken us so long to get here."

"There's a shower just through that door," said the Professor. "No need to remove your clothes, just open the door marked 'Gooey Toffee Sticky Remover

Shower And Dryer-Metron'. Step in, and press the big red button with 'START' printed on it."

Treaclepops found the shower .. er .. Gooey Sticky Remover Thingy .. and stepped into it. In front of her was a big red button, so she pushed it.

WHOOOOOSH!

Everything began to vibrate, hot and cold air was blowing from all directions, her skin tingled and a lovely sensation swept over her whole body. It was like she was being totally refreshed inside and out.

"Ooh, what a thrill, I'm loving this!" sighed Treaclepops, "I'll have to get one of *these*."

After a few minutes the WHOOOOOSH subsided, and Treaclepops was left feeling brand new! She hopped out of the shower, and headed back to where the Professor was frantically waving his arms around and writing things on a blackboard.

"So you see .." he said, scribbling frantically on the board with a big piece of white chalk. There were arrows, x's, y's, and = signs everywhere. "I still need one part of the equation to complete the formula for the .. oh hello Treaclepops .. come in, come in and take a seat. I'm just explaining to Toppety here, that I need the last piece of the puzzle ...."

Toppety looked at Treaclepops as she sat down. "Wow!" he said. "That must have been some shower! You look lovely, like you've just been made."

Treaclepops blushed.

"Now listen you two, this is important!" the Professor said, making more chalk dust as he hastily rubbed something from the board to make a correction.

"For some time now Lolly Town has been getting warmer. We don't know why. My friends at the

Science Club are always arguing about it, putting forward different theories. Professor Ice-Hat Newstick says it's caused by nature, and it's just a natural occurrence we can't do anything about. But articles in the Daily Melt are always

saying that it is caused by something we are doing here in Lolly Town. Either way, we need to do something about it, so we can go out again. I don't want to be stuck in this house until my expiry date."

"So what can *we* do to help Professor?" said Treaclepops eagerly.

"Well, during the Lolly-Humbug war, way before you two were made, I had to go behind enemy lines with another lolly agent, my friend Spivey. It was Spivey the Miv and me, against the full might of the Humbug. I was a handsome young lolly back then. The Humbug lived in warmer places far away from Lolly Town, and so we needed something to keep us cool over there. We were issued with Secret Prototype Cooling Pants."

"Wow! How cool is that! Pants that keep you

cool." said Toppety. "Sometimes I get real hot in mine."

"Now, when we got back from our mission," continued the Professor raising his eyebrows at Toppety, "the Cooling Pants were so top-secret that we had to hand them back straight away. But I did notice that there was a label in the back that read 'Prototype by Annie Seedballs'. I've made some enquiries, and most of the wartime records have been destroyed. But someone from the Ministry told me that he saw Annie Seedballs recently, at The Old Sweets Home. Obviously I can't go there myself, so that's why I have called on you two to go for me. I've been able to make a pair, but they are not quite cool enough. I just need one last bit of the equation to make them work properly."

"So you want us to go to The Old Sweets Home, find Annie Seedballs, get her to give us the last bit of the equation and bring it back to you?"

"Yes, that's exactly what I want you to do Toppety, right away."

"Where is The Old Sweets Home?"

Professor Ice 'n' Stein went to the refrigerator and opened the door.

"Here is a map," he said reaching into the ice box and pulling out a sheet of ice.

Toppety and Treaclepops had never seen a map made from ice before.

"This shows you the way to go," said the Professor, "but you'll have to be quick before it melts."

"Let's go then Treaclepops," Toppety said, taking hold of her hand. "We'll do our best Professor."

The ice map was cold in his fingers, as they ran down the path from the house.

Chapter 5:

The Old Sweets Home

"Wow, you just don't realise what old timers have been through, do you Treaclepops?" said Toppety, as they began to follow the map's directions.

"I know what you mean, the Professor must have been very brave in the war."

The map had begun to drip. With each step they took it was melting more and more.

"I don't think the Professor could have thought this through, giving us a map that melts! I think we had better memorise the way Toppety, the map is getting smaller and smaller! Soon it won't be there at all!"

"It's not far now," said Toppety, the map sliding about in his hands. "It's just over that hill."

As the two friends came to the top of the hill, they saw a big mansion with a lovely big garden and fountains around it.

"What a beautiful place to live!" said Treaclepops running excitedly down the slope towards the home. A big sign in front of the house read: 'The Old Sweets

Home for Retired Confectionery'.

They held each others hand as they walked up the long, long drive towards the big house. As they got nearer, they heard music coming from an open door. They peeked inside. It was a lovely big ballroom. It had a stage with a big silver glitterball hanging over it. A very suave looking old sweet was on stage singing, with a glass in one hand and a microphone in the other, and old sweets were dancing on the dance floor. The suave looking sweet sang ..

"It's a Jelly Bean world in the Spring time ... in the Spring it's a Jelly Bean world .."

"Let's go and ask that nurse where Annie Seedballs is," said Toppety, enjoying the music and slowly swaying. "Say, isn't that Dean Marshmallow Treaclepops? A singer from the recent past?" Toppety impressed himself with his extensive knowledge, as usual.

"Yes it is, and he is just as handsome now as he was in all the old black and white photographs that I've seen of him," swooned Treaclepops gazing up at the stage.

Dean Marshmallow looked down at her and winked. He still had that old black magic and a little sparkle in his eye.

"Come on Treaclepops, there's no time for this. We're on a mission."

The nurse was very pretty.

"Can I help you at all?" she asked sweetly. "I'm Nurse Sweetheart." She held out her hand in a delicate fashion. Toppety didn't know whether to shake it or kiss it, so he took hold of the fingers and gave them a bit of a waggle.

Treaclepops giggled at his silliness.

"I wonder if you can tell us where we can find Annie Seedballs?" she politely asked.

"She's here somewhere," answered the nurse, looking around. "She's usually in here this time of day, and she wouldn't miss Dean Marshmallow, he's gorgeous isn't he?"

"Oh yes!" replied Treaclepops.

Toppety frowned, he was a little bit jealous, not that he would ever admit it. Dean Marshmallow was swivelling his hips and singing a Rock'n'Roll number and the whole place was a-rockin' and the floor was a- jumpin'!

"Hang on .. there she is .. dancing with Dr Rock." Nurse Sweetheart pointed to two sweets whooping it up in the middle of the dance floor. Dr Rock was swinging Annie Seedballs around, one way then the other, twirling and twisting. Toppety and Treaclepops looked on in amazement, as Annie slid between Dr Rock's legs and then jumped to her feet, and was then quickly slung over his shoulder and down between the Doc's legs again. Everyone was in a circle now, as they clapped the two swinging sweets jiving in the centre.

Treaclepops turned to Nurse Sweetheart. "Wow! they certainly know how to rock, is that how Dr Rock got his name?"

"I prefer to call him Dr Love. When he's dancing he's Dr Rock, but he's always Dr Love to me." Nurse Sweetheart blushed.

The music came to an end with Dean Marshmallow doing the splits, while singing a very high note, miraculously managing not to spill any of his drink. All the sweets whistled and clapped.

"How does he do that?" Treaclepops asked in amazement.

"I don't know, but he does it every performance, he never misses that high note."

Dean took one last bow and he was gone.

"I'll introduce you to Annie," said Nurse Sweetheart, as she took them both by the hand, and led them to where Annie was busy taking compliments on her dancing from all the other sweets.

"You sure ripped up the floor Annie! You were brilliant"

"Thanks Dolly Mixture," said Annie, catching her breath.

Treaclepops suddenly noticed a fluffy mist in front of her eyes. "Toppety," she whispered, "what's that?"

"I don't know, Treaclepops," Toppety replied, rubbing his eyes and blinking, trying to focus.

Through the fluffy mist a voice complimented Annie, and two eyes blinked. "Yeah, you were great Annie, I loved watching you twirl, I love it when you ..."

Toppety and Treaclepops could now see it was a sweet covered in fluff. The sweet spun around copying Annie's moves. He twirled in front of Annie, then twirled off into the fuzzy distance. Behind him he left a trail of fluffiness, which he swept up with a little broom as he disappeared.

"That's Lozzy the Fluff," said Nurse Sweetheart.

"He's the caretaker. He's an ex-pocket sweet. Poor thing, never got rid of the fluff."

"You can't you know," confirmed Annie.

Nurse Sweetheart smiled warmly. "Annie, I want you to meet these two lovely young sweets, Toppety and Treaclepops."

"Well, what do we have here?" asked Annie. "What are two young sweets like you doing in a place like this? You have to be past your sell-by-date to get in here!"

Toppety put on his serious face.

"Well Miss Seedballs, we are on an urgent life or death mission on behalf of the lollies. Lolly Town is getting warmer and the lollies are melting, and we've come to see you to ask for your help."

"My help? I don't get around much these days

you know ..."

"Well, Professor Ice 'n' Stein told us that you ..."

"Ahh, dear Bertie he is such a dear lump of ice ... I remember when I first set eyes on him ... he was so, well you know ....."

"Well," continued Toppety, "he told us that during the Great Humbug war you invented Cool Pants, so that the lollies could infiltrate the hot Humbug enemy territory. He needs the last bit of your equation so that he can make Cool Pants and give them out to all the lollies."

"I can do better than that! After the war the Lolly Ministry Of Defence hid all the Cool Pants I made, so that if we ever needed them again, they would be ready."

"Oh wow!" said Treaclepops. "Where are they Annie?"

"Well, you know the cemetery at the edge of Lolly Town .."

"Oh no, not the cemetery!" said Treaclepops, her knees beginning to knock.

"Yes, the cemetery, well, there is a large statue of a white angel near the gate."

"Yes, yes we know it!" said Treaclepops.

"The Cool Pants are hidden inside there."

"Inside?" said Toppety. "It looked pretty solid to me!"

"Well, the base is hollow and that's where you'll find them. The angel is holding a wand. You need to take that down, take the star from the end of the wand, and place it in the star-shaped hole at the back of the base. Then put the wand through the middle of the star and turn it. Then it will open!"

"Wow! That's amazing!" said Treaclepops. "Just like adventures on the tele."

"Yes," said Toppety, "except this one is real! C'mon Treaclepops let's go!"

Toppety and Treaclepops thanked Annie Seedballs for all her help, and then they set off for the cemetery.

Chapter 6:

Sounds like a plan to me

Treaclepops and Toppety headed for the cemetery and the statue of the 'White Angel'. Excited by Annie's tale of intrigue and adventure, they skipped, jumped and sang their way down the path from the Old Sweets Home through the gate and out into the green meadow.

"Well Toppety only one more thing to do to complete our mission. Doesn't it feel great to do something good and help the lollies? Better than sitting at home on the sofa and watching TV?"

"Oh yes!" replied Toppety. "Although I do love those quizzy game shows where I can test my intelligence against the best in the world. One day I'm going to get myself on one of those and win a lot of money Treaclepops. Then when we're rich, we can just sit on the sofa and watch quizzy game shows without a care in the world!"

Treaclepops looked puzzled. "But isn't that what we do now Toppety?"

"Yes, I suppose it is Treaclepops, it's a funny old world isn't it!" They both laughed and took each other by the hand and skipped and jumped some more.

It wasn't long before they could see the White Angel in the distance. The wand she held high in her right hand was the first thing they saw.

"C'mon Treaclepops, we're nearly there. Let's do longer skips and jumps and we'll be there quicker."

They reached the gate to the cemetery, and to their horror, they saw Chocco Rocko sitting on the base of the statue.

"Oh No! There's Chocco Rocko, and look who's with him ...Almondo, Caramella's brother, and there's Caramella sitting under that tree. Who is that other sweet throwing your hat around?"

"Oh, that's Nutzerello, he's a nasty piece of sweet. Look how he's treating my hat, no respect at all."

Nutzerello was throwing Toppety's hat at the statue, trying to land it on the Angel's head. Treaclepops stamped her feet on the floor, reminding herself that Caramella was still wearing her pink boots.

"She's got a nerve, hasn't she Toppety, wearing my boots. Pink doesn't even suit her!"

"Don't get upset Treaclepops, remember the lollies, their problems are much bigger than ours, we must get those Cool Pants."

"But how?" sighed Treaclepops.

"Well .. you could sing one of your lovely lullabies Treaclepops, and that would put them to sleep, and then I could creep up, climb the statue, get the wand and be the hero!"

"That sounds like a good idea Toppety, but *you* love to go to sleep listening to my beautiful singing voice. I would put you to sleep too, and then where would we be?"

"You're right, Treaclepops, it was a silly idea. I would be in sleepy-by-land and we'd never get the Cool Pants. We'll have to think of something else."

They were both hiding under a tree so as not to

be seen, when an apple fell on Toppety's head.

"Ouch that hurt!" cried Toppety! "But it's given me an idea! We could throw apples at them. Going by the one that just fell on my head, they are pretty hard, and Chocco and his gang would run away."

"No Toppety, we don't want to hurt them, that wouldn't be very nice would it? You wouldn't like apples being thrown at you would you?"

"No Treaclepops, you're right, I wouldn't! Let's think some more."

 They both sat under the tree thinking thinking thinking and then thinking some more. Toppety was running his hands through his hair.

"Oh, if I only had my hat," he sighed, "I could think

of a brilliant idea!"

"Aren't you going to take your shoes off Toppety? Aren't you always telling me you have better ideas with your shoes off?"

"I've stopped doing that Treaclepops, I think it was just a bit silly."

They thought some more, thinking thinking thinking! Toppety took his shoes off anyway, desperately hoping for some inspiration.

"I've got a brilliant idea!" Treaclepops cried. "It came to me when you took off your shoes, and I saw your socks Toppety."

"So my socks are magic socks after all Treaclepops! I knew they were special, they just needed time to work."

"Yes, it is your socks! They reminded me of Caramella's best friend Tutti Fruiti, the same yellow and orange stripes as she has! Tutti lives in Lolly Town, and I'm sure if we tell Caramella that we are helping the lollies, and why we need to get to the White Angel, I'm sure she will help us."

"But how are we going to speak to Caramella without Chocco, Almondo and Nutzerello catching us Treaclepops?"

"*We* aren't going to speak to her Toppety, *you* are! You know when we're at home, that you love creeping up on me, and playing hide and seek? Well just imagine you're playing at home and you've got to sneak up behind Caramella. See, she's sitting in front of that tree, if you creep up and get behind the tree you'll be able to talk to her without the other three hearing you. Just tell her the whole story, and once she realises her best friend Tutti Fruiti is in trouble I'm sure she'll help."

"Okay Treaclepops, leave it to me! I'll hop, skip and jump, and then crawl to where she is .. tell her the whole story ... she'll get rid of Chocco, Almondo and Nutzerello .. then I'll call for you! I'll climb to the top of the White Angel, get the wand, unlock the base, and we'll have all the Cool Pants we'll ever need! Sounds like a plan to me Treaclepops!"

Toppety sat down and pulled his shoes back on.

"Wish me luck Treaclepops."

"Good luck Toppety, I know you can do it!" Treaclepops leaned forward and gave Toppety a little kiss on the cheek.

Then he was on his way, gliding from one bush to another, taking care not to be seen. He was quite close to Caramella now, just one more bush between him and the tree where she was sitting. Toppety took a deep breath and made a dash for the tree. He was there and no one had seen him.

"Pssst . . . Caramella," whispered Toppety.

She couldn't hear him. She was humming to herself.

He would have to reach around the tree, he thought, and tap her on the shoulder to get her attention. He could see Nutzerello still flinging around his beautiful hat, trying to get it on to the Angel's head. 'He's so useless,' Toppety thought to himself, 'I could have it on her head in one shot.' Chocco Rocko was sitting on the base of the Angel laughing at Nutzerello's stupid antics. Almondo was shooting blankly into the air with his catapult.

Toppety reached around the tree and tapped Caramella on the shoulder.

"Psst . . . Caramella . . . it's me . . . Toppety!"

Caramella jumped. "Oh my!" she said. "You gave me a fright!"

"Sorry! Please don't tell Chocco I'm here! I need your help, it's a matter of life and death for the lollies, but you must be very quiet and listen."

Caramella looked startled. "What do you mean life and death for the lollies?" she whispered.

"The lollies are in trouble! I know your best friend is Tutti Fruiti, well, the lollies are melting and so I need to get to the statue of the White Angel to save them ..."

"The lollies are melting? Oh dear me, that means Tutti's orange stripes will mingle with her yellow stripes and that won't be a good look at all!"

"It's worse than that," continued Toppety. "They melt completely, into a pool of water on the floor!"

"Oh my goodness! What is to be done?" cried Caramella dismayed at the thought of Tutti Fruiti as a small puddle.

"Shhh!" whispered Toppety trying not to be noticed. "Listen, I need to get to the White Angel, can you distract Chocco and his friends, or get rid of them altogether?"

"Are you sure the White Angel has the answer? Is it going to talk to you?"

"No, silly, as if it can *talk* to me!" poo-poohed Toppety, giving her a look of disbelief at such a silly idea, conveniently forgetting that most of his ideas are just as silly! "The White Angel has Cool Pants and I need to get them."

Caramella burst out laughing! "She has what?"

"Cool Pants!" insisted Toppety still trying to be as quiet as possible.

"That's what I thought you said!" She burst out laughing again. "But she's not wearing any pants! Tee hee tee hee tee hee . . ."

"No, silly, she's got them in a drawer in the base. I need them for the lollies to wear so that they won't melt, and they'll stay cool in the Cool Pants."

"So you're telling me that the White Angel has got Cool Pants in her drawers!"

"Yes, yes, Caramella, that's exactly what I'm saying. But I can't get to them while Chocco and his mates are there."

"Oh I see," replied Caramella.

"Finally!" exclaimed Toppety, taking a deep breath.

"Well you must admit it's a strange story to spring on someone!"

"I know, but it's all true. Can you help me?"

"Yes, but how can I get rid of them? They are having such a good time playing on the statue."

"We need a good idea! I'm very good at those, so hang on a minute." Toppety did his usual thinking thinking thinking. "Perhaps we could scare them away?" he finally said in a whisper.

"Yes, they may look tough, but they're cowards really. I'm sure we can scare them away. But how?" she pondered. "Maybe my idea about the White Angel talking isn't so silly after all. If we could make it speak that would scare them, and I bet they'd run a mile. But how?"

"I could do my special ventriloquist act! I learnt it one afternoon when I was watching the tele. All I'll have to do is get behind that tree, near the statue, and I'll be able to throw my voice, and it will be just as if the White Angel is talking! You distract them Caramella, while I creep round to the tree."

"Okay Toppety, good luck."

Caramella skipped towards the unsuspecting trio and grabbed Toppety's hat from Nutzerello. "Give that to me you silly! You'll never get it on the Angel's head. Let me try."

Caramella tossed the hat through the air and it landed squarely on the head of the White Angel.

Nutzerello didn't look very pleased, but Chocco Rocko and Almondo laughed and laughed. Their laughter soon ended when a spooky voice called out to them.

"Nutzerellooo .... Almondooo ... Choccoo Rockoooo, I've had enough of your silly games, this hat on my head is the last straw .. If you haven't disappeared by the time I count to three, I'll be very, very angry! One .... Two ..... "

Chocco, Almondo and Nutzerello looked terrified and they quivered with fear. They jumped on their bikes and sped off into the woods as fast as their pedals could take them.

Caramella laughed. "We did it Toppety! They won't be back in a hurry!"

Toppety popped his head out from behind the

tree to see the dust from the bicycle wheels disappearing into the distance.

"Hooray!" he exclaimed excitedly, and rushed to the White Angel. Climbing to the top, and waving to Treaclepops on the way up, he popped his hat back on his head. He carefully removed the wand from the White Angel's hand, and sliding back down the statue, he hit the ground with a bump.

"Ouch! That hurt! I keep doing that!"

Treaclepops arrived and gave him a big hug. "My hero!" she cried wrapping her arms around him.

Toppety slowly pulled the star from the wand.

"Hurry up Toppety! Hurry up!" said Treaclepops. "Here's the place where the star fits. Put it in, put it in!"

Toppety placed the star into the star-shaped hole

at the back of the statue. Then he took the wand and pushed it into the centre of the star.

Both Caramella and Treaclepops were now skipping and jumping around Toppety, as he knelt down and started to turn the wand. Three turns later the door popped open. There were all the Cool Pants toppling out on to the ground.

"It's true!" cried Caramella. "It's true!"

"Hurray!" shouted Treaclepops, and she and Caramella hugged each other, before realising that they didn't really like each other, and tumbled apart.

"This is silly," said Caramella, "I'm so sorry Treaclepops. I had no idea you were on a mission to save the lollies. Here, have your lovely pink boots back, and I hope we can be friends."

Treaclepops was overjoyed to get back her prized pink boots. She put them on and skipped and jumped around.

"Help me pick up all the Cool Pants," said Toppety, gathering as many as he could into his arms. "We'll never carry all of these, there's way too many."

"Toppety, I think I saw a wheel-barrow in the cemetery .." said Treaclepops.

"That could have been one of my ideas Treaclepops, it was so good! Let's go and get it."

The wheel-barrow was upside down next to one of the headstones.

"We can bring it back later, when we have finished with it," said Toppety wheeling it back to the statue.

After throwing all the Cool Pants into the wheelbarrow, they waved goodbye to Caramella and headed back down the road to Lolly Town.

"Don't forget the yoyo competition!" Caramella shouted after them.

"I won't!" replied Toppety, turning to see her doing a 'loop the loop'.

Chapter 7:

Cool Pants to the Rescue

Professor Ice 'n' Stein was very pleased to see them indeed, and even more pleased to stack up the Cool Pants on his kitchen floor.

"I'll make sure the lollies get these straight away," he said. "You two have saved the day!".

"Annie sends her love, Professor," said Treaclepops

"Oh!" said the Professor blushing scarlet.

"I'm sure she'd be really pleased to see you, now that you can go out again. She seems to have a very soft centre for you!"

"Yes, well .. erm, I think I will go and see her very soon, and thank her personally. But first I will have to get these Cool Pants to all the lollies in Lolly Town."

Toppety picked up a pair of Cool Pants. "Can we take this pair for Licky Lolly? She is in our ice cube tray."

"Oh my goodness!" exclaimed the Professor. "Yes, yes, you must get her into those straight away. Oh .. and take this too, you'll need this to make Licky back into her lolly shape." The Professor handed Toppety a bag. "The instructions are inside, it's quite simple, just pull the string .. but make sure she's thawed out before you try it."

Treaclepops and Toppety left the Professor waving to them from his doorstep, wearing his new Cool

Pants and a big smile.

The two friends hopped, skipped and jumped their way back home, and it seemed like no time at all before they were back at number 13 Sweetwrapper Lane. Treaclepops opened the gate.

"Isn't it lovely to be back home?" she said skipping up the path.

"Yes it certainly is," replied Toppety. "Just one last thing to do and our mission is complete."

Toppety and Treaclepops wasted no time at all in getting Licky out of the fridge. Toppety got his favourite hot water bottle that he likes to cuddle when he's not feeling too well.

"This will do nicely," he said, filling it with warm water. "This'll warm Licky up!"

Treaclepops placed the ice cube tray on top of the hot water bottle and in no time at all, Licky was liquid again.

Toppety opened the bag the Professor had given him. Inside was a yellow cube with a string attached. On the side was some writing, it read:

'INSTRUCTIONS: PULL THE STRING AND STAND WELL BACK ...OH .. AND WATCH OUT FOR THE STICK!'

"Well, this is new, isn't it Treaclepops? We've never done this before. We'd best do as it says and stand well back .."

Toppety pulled the string.

ZWhooosh!

The yellow cube turned into a lolly-shaped container, and a wooden stick sprung out from one end. Toppety jumped out of the way just in time. The stick missed his nose by inches.

"Ooo-er . . I nearly had a stick up my nose! Well I never," he said, amazed at the ingenious rubbery contraption. "Let's put Licky in."

They both took hold of the ice cube tray and carefully poured Licky into the lolly-shaped space. Nothing seemed to happen.

"What do we do now Toppety?" said Treaclepops, looking around for a switch or a button to press. "Were there any other instructions in the bag?"

Toppety looked inside the bag. "Oh yes, here they are!"

"Well that's just like you isn't it Toppety? You always start something before you have read the instructions properly."

"Well I've got them now, hang on a minute ..."

Treaclepops grabbed the piece of paper from his hand. "Here, give them to me, I will read them properly."

Treaclepops read the instructions very carefully. "I've found the bit we need Toppety, there should be a big red button on the side, marked: 'PRESS TO START'. Can you see it?"

Toppety started looking. "Ah, here it is Treaclepops, it was hiding under the stick, no wonder we couldn't see it."

"Well, don't do anything yet Toppety, just let me finish reading the instructions." Treaclepops finished reading the instructions. "Press the button!" she announced.

Toppety pressed the button, and the room was lit up with a blue flash as the lolly-making machine re-made Licky.

"Where am I? What happened?" Licky said, as she sat up and blinked.

"Oh Licky, we're so pleased to see you!" Treaclepops cried, giving her a big hug.

"Oh I remember," said Licky, "I was melting wasn't I? And you were going to save the lollies weren't you . . . did you . . is everything all right?"

"Yes, yes," said Treaclepops, "here, quickly put on these Cool Pants. They stop you from melting."

"What ....? Cool Pants!"

"Yes, Cool Pants, it's a long story Licky, and

yes, everything is fine now, and you wouldn't believe how we did it ... we had quite an adventure didn't we Toppety?"

"Yes, yes we did, you see, after we put you in the ice cube tray we set off for Lolly Town to see Professor Ice 'n' Stein just like you said . . ."

"And I put on my pink non-stick boots, didn't I Toppety . . . and I got stuck in a big puddle of gooey toffee sticky stuff, didn't I Toppety . . . oh, but hang on a minute ... what's the time?" Treaclepops looked at her watch. "Oh, it's 4.15 Toppety, our favourite programme's just starting ... Who wants to win a lot of money?"

"Let's go and watch it then Treaclepops, c'mon Licky, and afterwards we'll tell you all about our adventure."

The End

Hello Readers,

Toppety and Treaclepops like to stay out of the limelight and don't want their faces splashed all over the celebrity magazines. For this reason we haven't printed their pictures in this book, so they can remain anonymous when out in public.

Toppety and Treaclepops think it would be fun to know what you think they look like. Please send your drawings of them to the email below, and we will post the best ones on their Sweetville website.

See you soon for a new adventure . . .

Email your pics to us at: sweetville@live.co.uk

Visit Sweetville at: www.sweetvillepress.com